RACE CARS

Written by
PENNY WORMS

Smart Apple Media

Published by Smart Apple Media,
an imprint of Black Rabbit Books
P.O. Box 3263, Mankato, Minnesota 56002
www.smartapplemedia.com

Published by arrangement with Watts Publishing, London.

Cataloging-in-Publication Data is available from the
Library of Congress
ISBN: 978-1-59920-992-0   (library binding)
ISBN: 978-1-68071-011-3   (eBook)

The author would like to thank Felix Wills and the
following for their kind help and permission to use
images: Jeremy Davey from the Thrust team; Dave
Rowley from the Bloodhound team; and the media
teams at Audi, BMW and McLaren.

Picture Credits
Audi (UK): 7b, 15b, 16/17 (all images). BMW AG: 12/13.
Car Culture/Corbis: chapter page, 14/15, 19b. Carolyn
Kaster/AP/Press Association Images: 19t. Chris Wright,
www.bangerracing.com: 20/21 (all images). Getty Images:
18 (for NASCAR), 22. Jamie Duff/Press Association
Images: 13r. Jeremy Davey: 26l, 27r. Martin Rickett/PA
Wire/Press Association Images: 6/7. McLaren, www.
mclaren.com: title page, 8/9, 8b. PA/Press Association
Images: 14l. Shutterstock: 10/11 (all images), 23t,
23b, 25. Sutton/Press Association Images: 9b. www.
bloodhoundssc.com: 26/27. www.carphotolibrary.co.uk:
24t, 25b.

Printed in the United States by CG Book Printers
North Mankato, Minnesota

Disclaimer: Some of the "Stats and Facts" are
approximations. Others are correct at time of writing, but
will probably change.

PO 1728
3-2015

CONTENTS

MOTOR RACING

Motor racing has been around for over 100 years. Since cars were invented, the makers and owners have wanted to see whose car is better or faster. Now motor racing is a worldwide sport, with people racing just about every kind of car.

SPEED

Some racing is all about speed. Cars built for drag racing and Formula One are designed to be fast, but it's not always the fastest that wins a race. It's the car that crosses the finish line first.

ENDURANCE

Some races are long and tough. Rally racing and long-distance races require cars that are built to overcome difficult challenges.

TEAMWORK

At the top level, motor racing is about serious sport and serious money. At the lowest level, it is mostly about fun. Usually there is a team involved, whether professionals (left), or father and son. Often one person is the driver and the others build and maintain the vehicle. It's sport at its dirtiest, loudest, and most exciting.

FORMULA ONE CAR

Formula One cars are the ultimate racing machines. Designed with only one seat for the driver, they are built using the most advanced **technology** and **engineering**. The teams spend millions of dollars trying to make their cars the fastest on the track.

McLaren Mercedes MP4-24

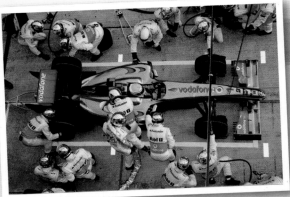

PIT STOP

Formula One cars are called open-wheel racers because their wheels are outside the main body of the car. This means they can be changed quickly in the **pits**.

STATS AND FACTS

- **Car:** KF1 kart
- **Top speed:** 85 mph (140 km/h)
- **Race locations:** Worldwide
- **Cost:** About $3,000 new
- **Claim to fame:** Lewis Hamilton, 2014 Formula One World Champion, started out racing karts.

KF1

A KF1 kart has a 125**cc** engine. This number tells you how big the engine is. A small road car might have a 1200cc engine. This means that the kart's engine is far less powerful. However, a kart is much lighter than a car so it can reach high speeds more quickly.

WTCC RACER

Touring cars are road cars that have been adapted for racing on a track. The cars have the same bodies as cars you see on the road, but the engines are more powerful and the **cars** have been made strong enough for racing.

The track in Valencia, Spain

WTCC TRACK

The cars that race in the World Touring Car Championship (WTCC) are usually **hatchbacks** or **sedans** with 2000cc engines. The racing tracks are circular but have turns and straights.

STATS AND FACTS

- **Car:** BMW 320si WTCC
- **Top speed:** 52 mph (245 km/h)
- **Race locations:** Worldwide
- **Cost:** $115,000
- **Claim to fame:** The most successful car in recent WTCC history.

WHEEL-TO-WHEEL COMBAT

What is exciting about touring car racing is that, beneath the stickers and spoilers, these are cars you see on the road. The difference on the track is that they are going at high speed, nudging one another, and overtaking in wheel-to-wheel combat. To many fans, this is "real" motor racing.

BMW

The BMW 320si (left) has been the most successful car in recent WTCC history, and touring car racing is BMW's most successful sport. The 320si road model was developed alongside the racing model (opposite).

LE MANS RACER

In the late 1950s and early 1960s, Ferrari cars reigned supreme in motor racing. The Ferrari 250 Testarossa remains one of the most **iconic** racing cars of all time. Its design was much more beautiful and different from other sports cars at the time.

24 HOURS OF LE MANS

Le Mans is one of the toughest, oldest car races in the world. The drivers race on the roads of Le Mans in France for 24 hours straight (day and night). A Testarossa won it in 1958, 1960, and 1961. Back then, drivers had to run to their cars at the start.

TODAY'S LE MANS

Today's Le Mans cars are **prototypes** built specially for the race. In 2008, the Audi R10 TDI was the first diesel car to win. It used 11 gallons (41 litres) of fuel per 62 miles (100 km) and only needed 30 minutes in the pits over the entire 24 hours.

STATS AND FACTS

- **Car:** Ferrari 250 Testarossa
- **Top speed:** 168 mph (270 km/h)
- **Race location:** France
- **Cost:** $40,000 in 1958–1959
- **Claim to fame:** In 2009, a Testarossa sold for over $12.2 million, the highest price ever paid for a car.

FERRARI 250 TESTAROSSA

Fenders

According to one of the original car's builders, the idea for the shape of the Testarossa was taken from the Formula One cars of the time. Ferrari introduced the rounded **fenders** to bring air into the body to cool down the brakes.

GT RACER

The Audi R8 LMS is Audi's newest GT3 racer. GT stands for "Gran Turismo" and GT3 is the most recent category in the GT race series. GT3 cars are based on standard two-seater sports cars. The R8 LMS is an "**off-the-shelf**" racer, perfect for those who want to race, but Audi is producing road models, too.

Audi R8 LMS GT3

BRAND-BUILDING

Many of the top sports car **brands** compete with Audi in the GT series, including Ferrari, Porsche, Lotus, BMW, and Aston Martin. They develop their road cars in line with their racing cars, and success on the track raises a company's profile and makes its road cars more desirable.

STATS AND FACTS

- **Car:** Audi R8 LMS GT3
- **Top speed:** over 200 mph (322 km/h)
- **Race locations:** Europe
- **Cost:** around $136,000 new
- **Claim to fame:** Based on the R8 Le Mans car which won the 24-hour race five times in 2001 to 2006.

SAFETY

A big concern when building any car is safety. It is even more important in racing cars because high-speed crashes are common. Racing cars have in-built **roll cages** and **cross bracing**. Both protect the driver if the car rolls over or crashes.

INSTANT GEAR SHIFTS

The R8 LMS has six gears and the driver changes gear by tapping a paddle on the steering wheel rather than using a gear stick. Low gears are used around corners. High gears are used along straights.

STOCK CAR

Stock car racing is the most popular form of racing in the United States. NASCAR is the ruling body and they decide how the cars should be built for each race series. The top series is the Sprint Cup, and all cars must be American-made and built to a specific CoT design (Car of Tomorrow). This makes the races very competitive.

THE CAR OF TOMORROW

NASCAR changed the design for the Sprint Cup racers to make the cars slower, safer, and cheaper to run. Because of the strict rules, each competitor is driving the same style of car with the same size engine. Winning is more about their racing ability rather than their car's performance.

STATS AND FACTS

- **Car:** General Sprint Cup stock car
- **Top speed:** over 200 mph (320 km/h)
- **Race location:** USA
- **Cost:** over $150,000 (to build)
- **Claim to fame:** In 2007, a new world stock car speed record was set at 244.9 mph (394 km/h).

MANUFACTURERS

The four cars currently built for the Sprint Cup are the Toyota Camry, the Ford Fusion, the Dodge Charger and the Chevrolet Impala. The CoT models closely resemble the road-going **production cars.**

SIDE-TO-SIDE COMBAT

With over 40 cars on the **starting grid**, side-to-side contact is common. The cars are built with rails, bars, and steel plating on the driver's side. They also have special foam pads inside the doors that absorb the energy of an impact.

BANGER

anger racing usually takes place on short oval dirt tracks in Great Britain. Like other car races, the first car to finish wins. The difference is that drivers stop at nothing to get there. They push their own cars beyond their limits and try to get competitor's cars off the track. Wrecks are common!

RACE TO THE END

Some banger races are non-contact. Others are team races with two or four cars chained together. Often there is a demolition derby at the end. This is not really a race. The winner is the last car moving, having demolished the other cars.

SAFETY FIRST

The most important part of any banger is its roll cage. The cars often end up on their sides or upside down. There are no rules governing banger racing, so each driver needs to make sure they are fully protected.

STATS AND FACTS

- **Car:** General banger
- **Top speed:** up to 60 mph (100 km/h) on a clear track
- **Race location:** Great Britain
- **Cost:** probably no more than $1,000
- **Claim to fame:** There are more crashes in banger racing than any other motorsport.

BEST BANGERS

Bangers are often pieced together using spare parts from scrap cars. Small hatchbacks are the most common form of banger, but it is often hard to tell what the original car was under all the paint, plating, and dents.

DRAGSTER

Drag racing is the loudest motorsport on earth. Two cars race in a straight line over a set distance, usually a quarter of a mile (400 m). The first over the finish line wins. The fastest are Top Fuel dragsters. They go so fast they need parachutes to slow them down. They complete the quarter mile in less than 5 seconds.

ROCKET FUEL

Top Fuel dragsters run on a blend of fuel that is similar to rocket fuel. No wonder the cars can go almost as fast as jet planes. Racing Top Fuel dragsters is also very dangerous!

STATS AND FACTS

- **Car:** Top Fuel dragster
- **Top speed:** 330 mph (530 km/h)
- **Race location:** Worldwide
- **Cost:** approximately $250,000
- **Claim to fame:** The sound of Top Fuel drag racing can be heard over 8 miles (13 km) away.

STICKY TIRES

Before any drag race, the tires are heated up by what is called a "burnout." Water is sprayed onto the wheels and the driver presses the **throttle** hard for three seconds. The wheels spin, which heats up the rubber to make them sticky. This helps them to grip the track for a fast start.

FUNNY CARS

The other classes of drag racing include the Funny Car. These dragsters look a little like normal road cars but underneath they are super-charged speedsters!

RALLY CAR

Rally racing is the cross-country of motorsports. Races are on public and private roads or tracks, so rally cars need to be built for both. The Ford Focus RS is based on the production car but has been heavily adapted for this type of racing.

ALL CHANGE

The World Rally Championship is top-class rallying. It takes place over three days and on different courses. Some courses are snow and ice. Some are roads or gravel tracks. The car's **suspension** needs adapting for each race. A car's suspension connects a car to its wheels. It has **shock absorbers** and springs for a smooth ride and softer landings.

TURBOCHARGED

The Ford Focus RS rally car is specially built to cope with the tough courses. It is four-wheel-drive, meaning the engine drives all four wheels. Also, its engine is turbocharged to give it more **acceleration** and speed.

STATS AND FACTS

- **Car:** Ford Focus RS
- **Top speed:** 161 mph (259 km/h)
- **Race location:** Europe, Australia, and South America
- **Cost:** $40,000 (road car price)
- **Claim to fame:** In 2008, Jari-Matti Latvala (22) because the youngest driver to win a world rally.

FROM TRACK TO ROAD

Ford, like other car makers, races cars to learn lessons about performance and safety. They apply what they learn to their road cars.

LAND-SPEED CAR

In 1997, Thrust SSC broke the land-speed record with a top speed of 763.035 mph (1,227.985 km/h). It was officially the first car to travel faster than the speed of sound. Now the race is on to beat the record with Bloodhound SSC, the latest project from the Thrust team.

THRUST SSC

The world record was set in the Black RockDesert in Nevada. It is a dry lake bed and extremely wide and flat. Very few places on earth offer such a soft, smooth racing surface.

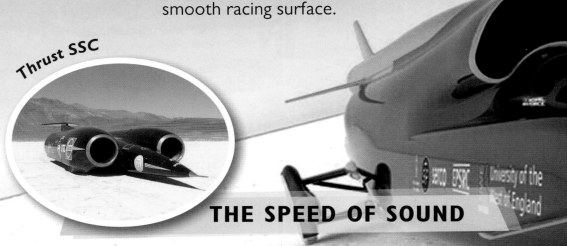

Thrust SSC

THE SPEED OF SOUND

The speed of sound is the speed at which sound travels through the air (around 750 mph or 1,236 km/h). When there is a loud noise in the distance, such as a car horn or an explosion, you don't hear it the instant it happens. It takes a little time for the sound to travel to your ears. So, Thrust was actually traveling faster than the noise it was making!

STATS AND FACTS

- **Car:** Thrust SSC
- **Top speed:** 763.035 mph (1,227.985 km/h)
- **Race location:** US
- **Cost:** Thought to be approx $6 million
- **Claim to fame:** Officially, the first **supersonic** car.

BLOODHOUND SSC

With Bloodhound SSC (Super Sonic Car), the aim is to reach a speed of 1000 mph (1,609 km/h) while controlling the car and keeping all four wheels on the ground.

Bloodhound SSC

At full speed Bloodhound will cover five football fields per second!

Thrust SSC was powered by two jet engines. Bloodhound SSC will use one jet engine to get to 350 mph (563 km/h), then a rocket to blast it to 1000 mph (1,609 km/h).

GLOSSARY

aerodynamic designed to travel through air easily at high speed

acceleration the rate at which a car builds up speed

brands what makes one type of car or product different and distinctive from another

cc cubic centimeters, the size of a car's engine. There are 16.4 cc in 1 cubic inch

cross bracing metal bars that go across the roll cage to make it even stronger

downforce the force caused by air rushing over a moving car that pushes it down onto a track or road

drag air movement around a moving car that pulls on the car and slows it down

engineering the use of science in designing and building engines

fenders guards over each wheel of a car

hatchbacks cars that have a lift-up door at the back

iconic something that, over time, has become an icon or symbol

off-the-shelf something that can be used as soon as it is bought and does not have to be changed or adapted in any way

pits the place on a race track where cars make quick stops for fuel or tire changes

production cars cars that are made in a factory and go on general sale

prototype a product made and used for testing before others are made, to see if it works and how it can be improved

roll cage a strong, metal frame built into a car that protects the driver if it crashes and rolls over

sedans family-sized cars with two or four doors and a trunk

shock absorbers air- or oil-filled car parts that soak up bumps in the road

starting grid the position of the cars at the start of a race

supersonic faster than the speed of sound

suspension a system of springs and shock absorbers that work between the body of a car and its wheels

technology the use of science and the latest equipment

throttle the pedal that is pressed to release fuel into the engine to make the car go faster.

INDEX